SURPRISE ISLAND

The Alden children are living happily with their grandfather now, but their adventures are just beginning!

Their first surprise is that they'll be spending summer vacation on their own private island. The island is full of surprises, including a kind stranger named Joe. Joe is always happy to help the children, but their new friend has a secret!

THE BOXCAR CHILDREN
GRAPHIC NOVELS

THE BOXCAR CHILDREN
SURPRISE ISLAND
THE YELLOW HOUSE MYSTERY
MYSTERY RANCH
MIKE'S MYSTERY
BLUE BAY MYSTERY

Gertrude Chandler Warner's

THE BOXCAR CHILDREN

SURPRISE ISLAND

Adapted by Rob M. Worley

Illustrated by Mike Dubisch

Henry Alden

Jessie Alden

Watch

Violet Alden

Benny Alden

Visit us at www.albertwhitman.com.

Adapted by Rob M. Worley
Illustrated by Mike Dubisch
Colored by Wes Hartman
Lettered by Johnny Lowe
Edited by Stephanie Hedlund
Interior layout and design by Kristen Fitzner Denton
Cover art by Mike Dubisch
Book design and packaging by Shannon Eric Denton

Library of Congress Cataloging-in-Publication Data

Worley, Rob M.
Surprise Island / adapted by Rob M. Worley ; illustrated by Mike Dubisch.
p. cm. -- (Gertrude Chandler Warner's boxcar children)
ISBN 978-1-60270-587-6
[1. Orphans--Fiction. 2. Family--Fiction. 3. Mystery and detective stories.] I. Dubisch, Michael, ill. II. Warner, Gertrude Chandler, 1890-1979. Surprise Island. III. Title.
PZ7.W887625Sur 2009
[E]--dc22

2008036100

SURPRISE ISLAND

Contents

THE FIRST SURPRISE
The four Alden children, Henry, Jessie, Violet, and Benny ran all the way home. Their grandfather, Mr. Alden, had promised them a surprise.
School is out for the whole summer!
Was this the day I said I'd tell you?
You said you'd tell us the minute school was out.
Once upon a time, my father bought an island.
He **bought** one!
Yes. A small one. If you want to stay there all summer you may.
Mr. Alden drove them to the ocean. Dr. Moore and his mother came along to enjoy the fun.
Captain Daniel will take us in the motorboat across to the island.

There's our island! Our very own island!
You children are going to live in the barn!
As soon as they landed, the children ran straight to the barn.
Bedrooms!
Let's bring down some straw for beds.
We can use these barrels and boards for a dinner table. Maybe I can make a cupboard for dishes.
I can cook plenty of things with this stove!
Henry can make anything!
While the children explored the barn, Captain Daniel asked Dr. Moore to look in on his friend.
He's a very handy man, Joe is, but he hasn't been well.
Last year, I fell and broke my arm. For a long time I didn't know who I was.
Do you remember who you are now?

Joe told Dr. Moore who he was. But Joe wanted it to be a secret.
Your secret is safe with me. Let me check your arm and be sure it is OK.

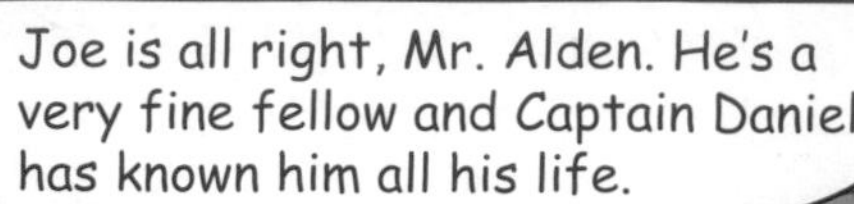

Joe is all right, Mr. Alden. He's a very fine fellow and Captain Daniel has known him all his life.

You're sure?
Yes. The children will like him.

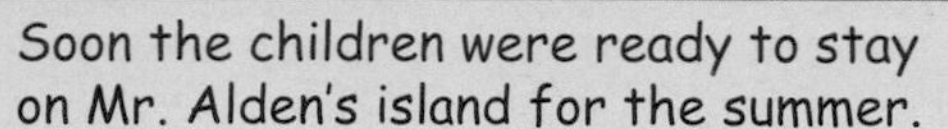

Soon the children were ready to stay on Mr. Alden's island for the summer.
Won't you be lonesome, Grandfather?
I need a little rest without any children or dogs around.
You won't hear Watch bark for a long time.

After taking Mr. Alden back home, Captain Daniel returned with supplies.

SUMMER PLAN
That night, the children ate dinner on the table that Henry had built. They washed their dishes in the spring outside. Then they went to bed.
Henry was the first to wake. He and Watch took a walk and were surprised by what they found nearby.
I wonder if this garden belongs to Captain Daniel.
How do you like your garden?
Our garden?
My name is Joe. I'm the handyman. Your grandfather had me plant it for you.
Look! We can have peas for dinner!
Henry, Jessie, and Violet picked peas. Joe had an important job for Benny.
Captain Daniel goes to the mainland every day. If you need anything, leave your order in this box.
This will be my job. I like to open the little door!

Henry, Jessie, and Violet had their own jobs to do.
How many places will we need in the cupboard, Jessie?
One shelf for spoons and things.
And one for pans and kettles, and one more for groceries.
And one shelf for dishes.
The morning passed quickly.

I made pea soup!
Oh boy!
The Alden children knew that everything seemed better when they had to work to get it.

After lunch, the children walked on the beach.
Jessie, look at that!
Clams!

Jessie and Henry brought spoons from the barn. Everybody dug for clams, even Watch.
I'm going to keep mine.
You won't want to keep them when you find out how good they taste.

I suppose these are for dinner tomorrow.
Yes. These will keep all right with seaweed on top.
The next day, there was even more to explore.
Look at this funny shell. It is just like a little boat.
And look at this pretty purple flower.
Let's save all the flowers and shells we find.
I have a great idea!
We can create a museum!
We are sure to find interesting things on this island to keep.
We'll find butterflies, birds, seaweed...
I think it's a wonderful idea.
We found these things without looking.

THE MUSEUM
Later, the children gathered the flowers, shells, seaweed, and driftwood they collected. Violet made a list for the museum.
How can I write the names of these flowers and shells when I don't know their names?
We could get books from the library.
I'll ask Joe to get them for us!
A few hours later, Joe arrived with books from the library.
Won't you stay for dinner, Joe?
You'll be our first guest, but you'll have to wash your own dishes.
Now show us the books, Joe!
Joe sure knows a lot about nature.
Joe and the children studied the new books. Joe seemed just as interested as they were.
How did you ever learn all this?
Oh, I just picked it up.

After Joe left, the Aldens went upstairs.
This is where we'll have the museum.
We can use this chair when Grandfather comes to visit.
Henry can build tables with these boards!
The next day, work on the museum began.
Joe gave me newspapers. And there was a box from Grandfather.
He sent sweaters!
Grandfather thinks it's going to get cold!
Now smooth the paper over the flower, like I learned in school.
What about the board?
We'll put the board over the paper, and the rock too. That way the flowers will be pressed flat as they dry.
Later it started raining. They spent the next day setting up the museum.

INDIAN POINT
The next day was warm again. The children went exploring.
What a big pile of shells!
It's taller than Benny!

Look, a little cave! Lets go in!

As they went farther into the cave they found several small rooms. Then Henry discovered something else.
It's an Indian arrowhead! What do you know?

WOOF! WOOF!
Something's wrong! Watch never howls!
WOOOOOOOOOO!
Henry! Water is coming into the cave!

The tide was coming in and filling the cave with water.
I'm scared of that old cave.
We're out, thanks to Watch!
Well I ought to have watched the tide. That cave is perfectly safe when the tide is out.

The children passed Captain Daniel's hut on their way to the barn.
Everything all right?
No! We're all scared and almost dead!
Captain Daniel has just made a big kettle of stew. Why don't you eat with us.

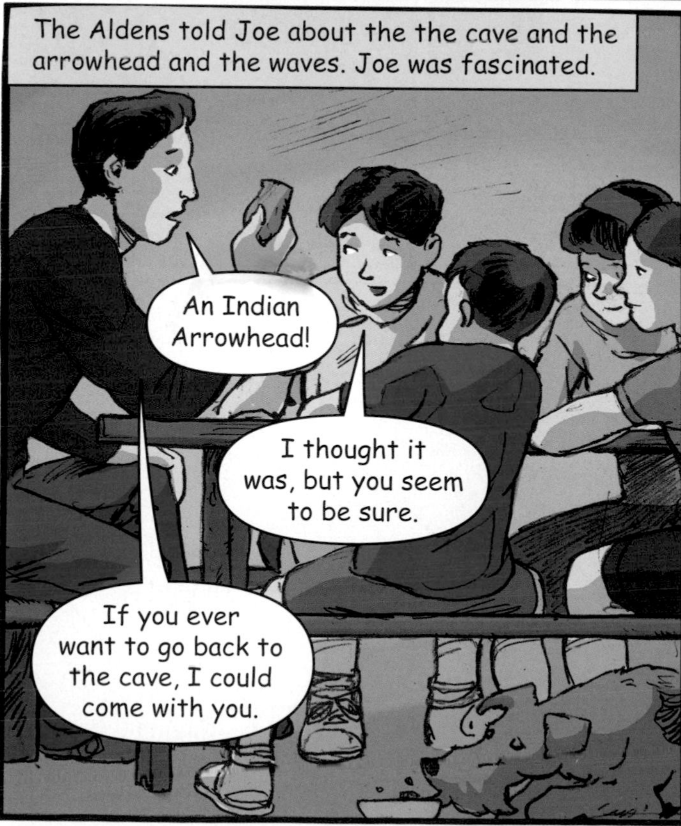
The Aldens told Joe about the the cave and the arrowhead and the waves. Joe was fascinated.
An Indian Arrowhead!
I thought it was, but you seem to be sure.
If you ever want to go back to the cave, I could come with you.

That would be great! There's a big pile of shells near the cave too!
What! A shell-pile? Then I will certainly go with you. I must!

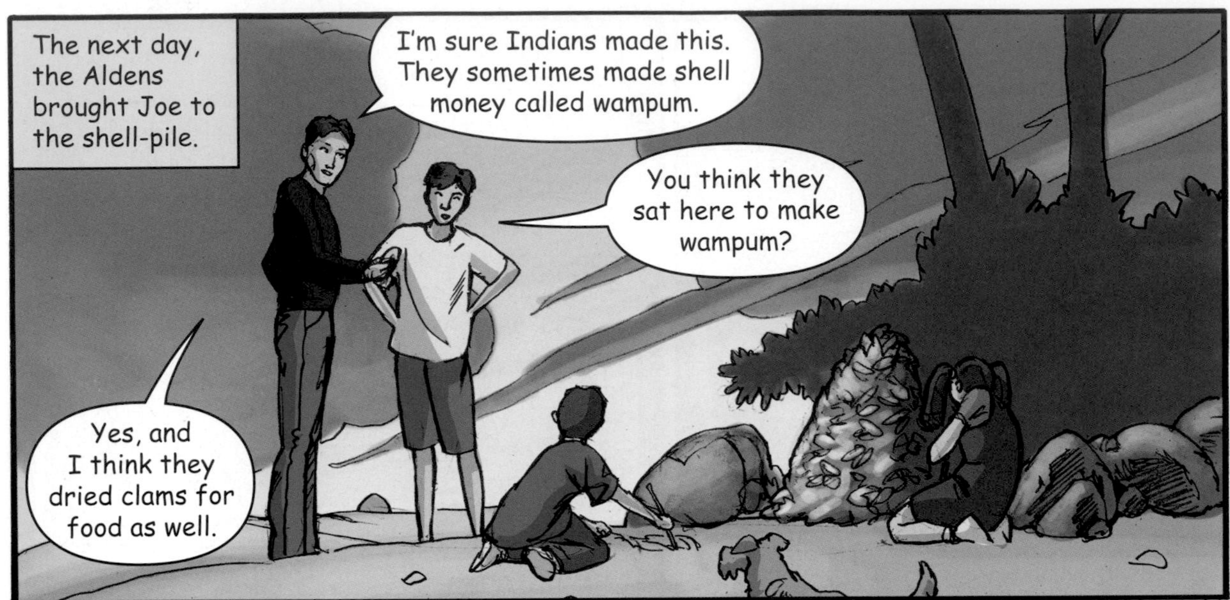
The next day, the Aldens brought Joe to the shell-pile.
I'm sure Indians made this. They sometimes made shell money called wampum.
You think they sat here to make wampum?
Yes, and I think they dried clams for food as well.

Joe, Henry, and Jessie went back for digging supplies. Benny and Violet were too tired, so they stayed at the shell-pile.

When Joe, Henry, and Jessie returned they had some clam hooks, a shovel, and a camera.
This picture will show how big the shell-pile is.

Joe began to dig carefully.
It isn't all fun. You may work for a year and not find anything.
I'd like to do this for a living--go to far-off places and dig up old things.
Just like fishing!

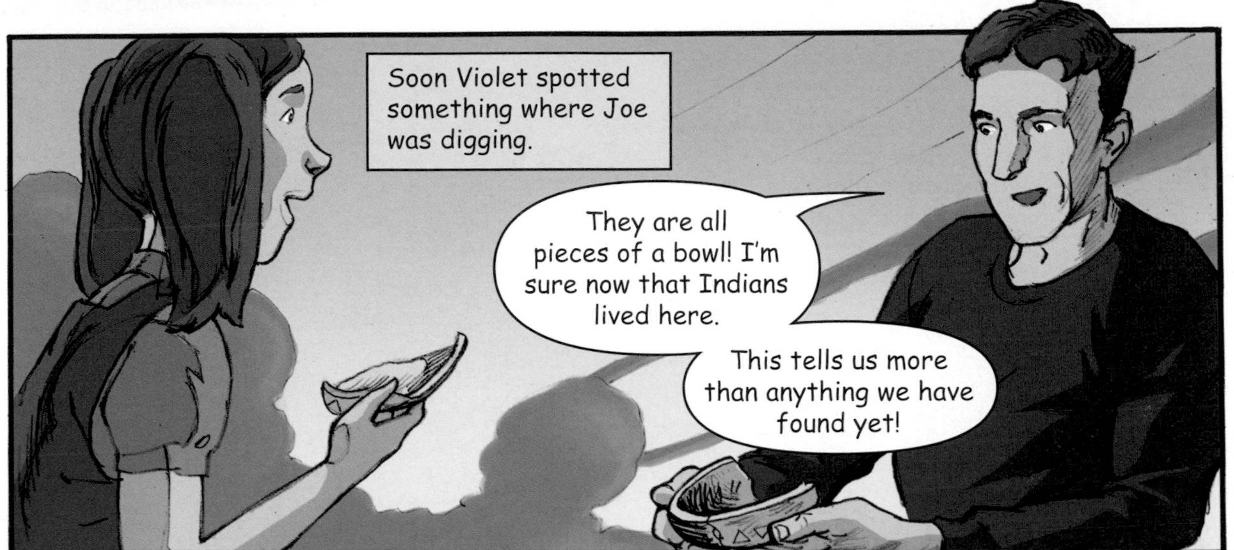
Soon Violet spotted something where Joe was digging.
They are all pieces of a bowl! I'm sure now that Indians lived here.
This tells us more than anything we have found yet!

Watch, there's a bone in your paw! It's made from animal bone!

That means Indians used to fish here, doesn't it? Let's call this end of the island "Indian Point."
I think so.

That night the children had trouble sleeping. The things they had found at Indian Point were very exciting. They had brought home the Indian bowl and put it in their museum.

VIOLINS AND VISITORS

After supper a few nights later, the children had another surprise. Violet heard music, and the children discovered Joe playing a violin.

Oh, **please** play it again! When did you learn to play? Could I hold it just a minute?

The children waited for a long time, but then suddenly...
What a big one!
I got one!
Many more of those and we'll be eating fish for a week!

Back home, Henry and Benny cleaned the fish.
I wish Grandfather could see these.
He's coming to visit us tomorrow. He telephoned Captain Daniel and said so.

Mr. Alden arrived the next day. The children were very excited to show him the museum.
The James H. Alden Museum
What's this I see? A museum?
Do you like it?
I like it very much indeed. It's the very thing I used to do myself.

I found a big bone near the shell-pile.
I remember seeing that shell-pile when I was a boy.
Joe helped us dig. We found all kinds of Indian things!

Grandfather joined the children for one of Jessie's meals.
What else do you have to show me?
I want you to see Joe. He's my best friend in all the world.
Well, after dinner I want to take you on a trip.

Have we left the island for good, Grandfather?
No, Benny. This won't take long. I want to show you something.
It's a museum! Look, Jessie!

THE ALDEN MUSEUM
My goodness! Is that named for you, Grandfather?
I suppose it is. It has been here a long time.
You gave them the money to build it!

The next morning it was very cold. But the children were excited about the museum Grandfather had shown them.
It's so cold today. Let's stay inside and paint our birds in our museum.

APPLE PIE

I'll cut out paper birds. You color them.

Cut out a picture of every bird we have seen. The bird book tells all the names.

I think Joe ought to have stayed here to see Grandfather.

A young man who went exploring for me last year has been lost.
Maybe you mean Joe. He has brown hair and brown eyes and a violin.
We think Joe is more than a handyman. He knows all about things on the island and all about Indians.
Indians! I **must** meet him.
Captain Daniel told me Joe has gone away for a day or two.
Then I will come back.
The next day, the Aldens put on a picnic. Captain Daniel brought the children's friends to the island.
Benny's friend Mike brought his dog, too.
Spotty is faster than Watch!
Oh no he's not!

Joe had returned much earlier than Captain Daniel had said. He made a fire so they could cook clam chowder for everyone.
Keep on eye on Benny and Mike, Henry.
They went over by those rocks.
We should check on them.

Look what we found!
I found it!
There's a paper inside the bottle. Let's take it out?

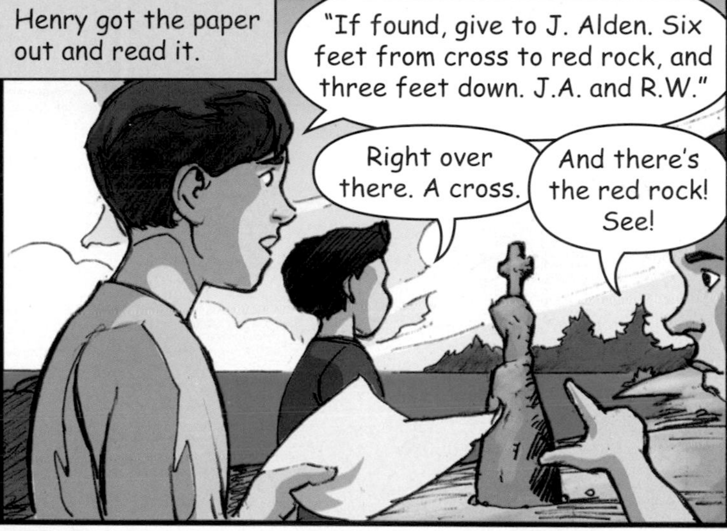
Henry got the paper out and read it.
"If found, give to J. Alden. Six feet from cross to red rock, and three feet down. J.A. and R.W."
Right over there. A cross.
And there's the red rock! See!

This will be easy. Joe said this string is six feet long.
Then this is the spot on the map. We should dig down three feet.

I'm getting tired.
Let's dig some other day.
It could be twelve feet down since the paper is very old.

Mike did not want to stop digging. Suddenly...
It's mine, all mine! You can't say it isn't, because you all stopped digging.
Five dollars! Grandfather will give you a new five dollar bill. He would like to keep this old money he put there as a boy.

Just as Mike smiled at the idea of a five dollar bill, Joe spotted something on the water.
There's somebody in the water!

Joe rescued the boy and pulled the boat ashore.
Joe is a great swimmer!
Everybody ought to know how to swim. That other boy just stood there and yelled.

What's the matter, Mike?
That's my brother, Pat! I told him about this picnic. Him and that boy Johnny stole a rowboat to come here in.
What an awful thing to do!
We won't ever take a boat again.
No, I don't believe you will either. I'll get you some dry clothes.
Pat and Johnny felt better after they ate. Everybody's spirits were up and they decided to play some ball.
Soon, Captain Daniel took the children home. Benny was sad to see Mike go.
Spotty can run faster than Watch!

Later Joe and Violet played their violins. It was the first time the children had heard Violet play since her lessons started.

Mr. Browning had returned, and he recognized Joe but he called him...
Mr. Browning!
JOHN!
I'm really glad to see you. Everything is all right again.
I wasn't well for a long time. Now I'm ready to go back to the museum.
He is the head of the Alden Museum!
My name is John Joseph Alden. I'm your cousin! I should like to come home with you and Uncle James if you'll have me.
Oh, Joe! I'd rather have you live with us than even Watch!
Benny called Grandfather and told him to come to the island. He didn't tell him why.
I don't think Mr. Alden had better see you suddenly, John.
Let Jessie fix it. I will stay in the hut until you tell me it's all right.

It's my birthday, Grandfather. I got lots of surprises today!
Oh no! Benny is going to tell Grandfather the secret!

This island is just full of surprises. We should call it Surprise Island!
Yes! Surprises like clams, and the violin...
...and the Indian things!

Are your veins all right, Grandfather?
My veins?
You know, some people have funny veins, so when they hear something awfully good, **suddenly,** they just drop down dead.
I am sure that good news wouldn't kill me.

Benny just made my job very easy, it seems.
What would be the best surprise you can think of?
The best surprise...would be a person.

John!
Uncle James!

Why didn't you come home, John?
I wanted to be well first. Then I met Dr. Moore and the children.

I got the best present for my birthday: a new cousin!
I feel as if it were my birthday.
It's everybody's birthday!
I think it's my birthday too.

Everybody is happy then. That's just right, because it's everybody's birthday.

GOOD-BYE SUMMER
Before they knew it, it was late summer.
I don't mind going home. I miss Grandfather.
We have to go home tonight.
I want to tell you something. I hope you won't feel bad about it.

I know you found the Indian things in the cave. But somebody ought to dig there who understands it.
Your Grandfather is letting a lot of men work with me here. Some days you'll be able to come and watch.
This sounded good to the children, especially Henry.

At their farewell dinner, Joe talked more about digging in the cave.
You found some wonderful things that will have to go to a museum even bigger than your Grandfather's.
I'd like to have this for my work, too! Can you teach me?
Yes, Henry. I'd like to.

Good-bye, Barn!
I am not going to cry.
Good for you, Benny! Just keep thinking how lonesome Grandfather has been.

Captain Daniel took the children to the mainland. When they saw their grandfather waiting, they ran to him.
Thank you for our summer on the island.
I'm glad you are all home. I shall even be glad to hear Watch bark tomorrow.
Soon they were ready to sleep in their regular beds again.
Joe is going to live with us, and he's my best friend in all the world.
I mean all but you, and Violet, and Henry--
And Watch?
Yes, of course Watch, and Grandfather--
Downstairs, the children's real best friend settled back in his big chair to make new plans for them.
MY ISLAND
BY

ABOUT THE CREATOR

Gertrude Chandler Warner was born on April 16, 1890, in Putnam, Connecticut. In 1918, Warner began teaching at Israel Putnam School. As a teacher, she discovered that many readers who liked an exciting story could not find books that were both easy and fun to read. She decided to try to meet this need. In 1942, *The Boxcar Children* was published for these readers.

Warner drew on her own experience to write *The Boxcar Children.* As a child she spent hours watching trains go by on the tracks near her family home. She often dreamed about what it would be like to live in a caboose or freight car—just as the Alden children do.

When readers asked for more Alden adventures, Warner began additional stories. While the mystery element is central to each of the books, she never thought of them as strictly juvenile mysteries. She liked to stress the Aldens' independence. Henry, Jessie, Violet, and Benny go about most of their adventures with as little adult supervision as possible—something that delights young readers.

During her lifetime, Warner received hundreds of letters from fans as she continued the Aldens' adventures, writing nineteen Boxcar Children books in all. After her death in 1979, her publisher, Albert Whitman and Company, carried on Warner's vision. Today, the Boxcar Children series has more than 100 books.